William Shakespeare's

THE TRAGEDY OF

Macbeth

Tamara Hollingsworth
and Harriet Isecke, M.S.Ed.

Publishing Credits

Dona Herweck Rice, *Editor-in-Chief*; Lee Aucoin, *Creative Director*; Don Tran, *Print Production Manager;* Timothy J. Bradley, *Illustration Manager*; Wendy Conklin, M.A., *Senior Editor*; Torrey Maloof, *Associate Editor*; Lesley Palmer, *Cover Designer;* Rusty Kinnunen, *Illustrator;* Stephanie Reid, *Photo Editor*; Rachelle Cracchiolo, M.A. Ed., *Publisher*

Image Credits

cover & p.1 *The Ghost of Banquo* by Theodore Chasseriau/Musee des Beaux-Arts, Reims, France/Lauros/Giraudon/The Bridgeman Art Library

Teacher Created Materials

5301 Oceanus Drive
Huntington Beach, CA 92649-1030
http://www.tcmpub.com
ISBN 978-1-4333-1272-4
©2010 Teacher Created Materials, Inc.
Printed in China

The Tragedy of Macbeth
Story Summary

In *The Tragedy of Macbeth*, three witches tell a general that he is destined to become King of Scotland. The general, Macbeth, becomes fixated on this prophecy. He and his wife decide to take matters into their own hands. At Lady Macbeth's urging, Macbeth begins murdering his way to the throne. When the pair finally gets what they want, they cannot enjoy it. Instead, they are crazed with guilt and paranoia.

Tips for Performing
Reader's Theater

Adapted from Aaron Shepard

- Do not let your script hide your face. If you cannot see the audience, your script is too high.

- Look up often when you speak. Do not just look at your script.

- Speak slowly so the audience knows what you are saying.

- Speak loudly so everyone can hear you.

- Speak with feeling. If the character is sad, let your voice be sad. If the character is surprised, let your voice be surprised.

- Stand up straight. Keep your hands and feet still.

- Remember that even when you are not speaking, you are still your character.

Tips for Performing
Reader's Theater *(cont.)*

- If the audience laughs, wait for the laughter to stop before you speak again.

- If someone in the audience talks, do not pay attention.

- If someone walks into the room, do not pay attention.

- If you make a mistake, pretend it was right.

- If you drop something, try to leave it where it is until the audience is looking somewhere else.

- If a reader forgets to read his or her part, see if you can read the part instead, make something up, or just skip over it. Do not whisper to the reader!

The Tragedy of Macbeth

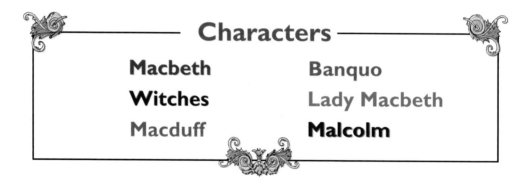

Characters

Macbeth	Banquo
Witches	Lady Macbeth
Macduff	**Malcolm**

Setting

This reader's theater is set in Scotland and England during the Middle Ages. It begins on a moor in Scotland, then moves to Inverness, Macbeth's castle, and later to the Palace of Dunsinane. A few scenes involving Macduff and Malcolm take place in England. The play concludes back at the Palace of Dunsinane.

Act I, Scene I

On a moor in Scotland

Macbeth: We fought our battles very well, Banquo. Between us, we have defeated the two armies that were invading Scotland.

Banquo: Yes, Macbeth, King Duncan will have much to celebrate. He will be pleased that his generals have had such great victories. He will be thrilled that we won against both the Irish and the Norwegians.

Macbeth: Banquo, do you hear those witches mumbling?

Witches: When shall we three meet again: in thunder, lightning, or in rain? Fair is foul and foul is fair. Hover through the fog and filthy air.

Macbeth: Did you hear that, Banquo?

Witches: A drum, a drum! Macbeth does come. All hail, Macbeth!

Macbeth: Why do you speak this way?

Witches:	We speak to you this way for we have important things to say. First, Macbeth will be the Thane of Cawdor, then he shall be king hereafter.
Banquo:	This is foolishness, Macbeth. Let us go and hear no more of this. Scotland already has a good and noble king.
Macbeth:	Wait, Banquo, this is curious. Witches, speak to me again. Tell me more of this future you see.
Witches:	Macbeth, we have told you your future. But just a moment, for we have more. Banquo's kings will be from his sons, though he himself will not be one.
Banquo:	This is too strange.
Witches:	All hail Macbeth and Banquo!
Banquo:	Are we both hallucinating, Macbeth?
Macbeth:	Perhaps we are, but I think it is best not to dwell upon these strange thoughts. Look! Here come the king's men to welcome us home.

Act I, Scene II

On the way to Macbeth's castle

Macbeth: The king's men said that because the last thane betrayed the king in battle, I will receive his title. Can you believe this, Banquo? I am to be the new Thane of Cawdor!

Banquo: How very strange that the witches' first prophecy seems to have come true, Macbeth.

Macbeth: Odd as it is, that does appear to be the case. But, I do have some trepidation, Banquo.

Banquo: What do you mean, Macbeth?

Macbeth: Do you think the second prophecy will come true, as well? Do you think that I shall become the next king of Scotland?

Banquo: We already have a good and honorable king. Do not wish him ill, Macbeth, for I fear evil will come to you if you do. This is all quite disturbing.

Macbeth: But if all the witches' prophecies come true, Banquo, you will have great joy. Remember, they said that your heirs will someday rule as kings.

Banquo: These are simply coincidences. You have received a reward from King Duncan. Take joy in that reward and think no more of the prophecies.

Macbeth: You are probably right, Banquo. But now I must write to my wife, Lady Macbeth. I must tell her about our strange conversation with the witches and have her ready our castle for the king.

Act I, Scene III

Later that day at Inverness, Macbeth's castle

Lady Macbeth: I know my husband is uncertain of the witches' prophecies, but the first one has already come true. We cannot let the next one slip by. King Duncan is staying at our castle tonight, and if we murder him while he is sleeping, my husband will become king. I shall go speak with him about my plan.

Macbeth: Hello, my dear wife. Is it not wonderful news that the battles have been won, and that I am now Thane of Cawdor?

Lady Macbeth: Indeed, it is. I have some strange and vexing thoughts I must reveal to you, my husband.

Macbeth: What is it, my dear?

Lady Macbeth: You must act to get what you want. I only wish I could move myself to feel no remorse against these deeds I want you to commit.

Macbeth: Deeds? What deeds do you speak of?

Lady Macbeth: The deeds that will make you king, of course. What are your thoughts?

Macbeth: The witches decreed my rise to royalty. However, I do not see a path to the crown without the destruction of my friend, King Duncan.

Lady Macbeth: Are you a child, a coward? If you know what you want, if you feel the crown upon your head, go and take it!

Macbeth: I do see the crown and even feel it upon my brow, but I do not know how the murder of Duncan sits with my soul.

Lady Macbeth: You are a pitiful man if you cannot act to get what you want! You have too much of a desire to do the right thing, to make the right choice. However, you can be an unstoppable force if you do as I say, for I have a plan that will get you what you truly want.

11

Macbeth:	What is your plan, my wife?
Lady Macbeth:	I will give the men who guard King Duncan many drinks at dinner to ensure that they pass out. When the king has fallen into a sound sleep, you will slip into his room and push a dagger straight through his heart.
Macbeth:	And then what will happen?
Lady Macbeth:	Then you will place the bloody dagger in the guards' hands and kill them. No one will doubt that the guards were the king's murderers. They will think that you dealt them a deathblow because of your anger against their terrible deed.

Act II, Scene I

That night at Macbeth's castle

Macbeth:	I have been thinking about what you said, my wife, but I am still not sure I can go through with these evil deeds.
Lady Macbeth:	Nonsense! The king must be fast asleep by now, and if you go quietly into his chamber and murder him, you will be crowned the new king.

Macbeth:	I do not know. My soul cries against it! But what if we should fail?
Lady Macbeth:	We fail? But screw your courage to the sticking place, and we will not fail!
Macbeth:	Yes, perhaps you are right.
Lady Macbeth:	The plan is foolproof, and the crown is completely within your grasp.
Macbeth:	I will be fulfilling the witches' prophecy, after all. Leave me alone with my thoughts, and I will follow the plan when I am ready.
Lady Macbeth:	Good night, my husband, soon to be king!
Macbeth:	What rights have I to the throne but seemingly crazy utterances of old witches? There is nothing in my blood but ambition that entices me to take this action. I am King Duncan's loyal general, his host, his friend, and he has done me no wrong, but still I seek his death. Passions, please leave me and let me feel nothing but the prophecy that proclaims me king. Is this a dagger which I see before me, the handle toward my hand? Come let me clutch thee. Now I must get hold of myself and complete what has been started.

Act II, Scene II

Early the next morning at Macbeth's castle

Lady Macbeth: I am glad to see you back in our chambers, my husband. Did everything go according to plan last night? You look pale. Are you all right?

Macbeth: I am shaken to the core. I heard King Duncan's sons saying their prayers as I was murdering their father. What a crime I have committed! I fear the worst may befall me now.

Lady Macbeth: Keep those foolish thoughts out of your head. Wait, what is this I see in your hand? Why have you brought this dagger dripping with blood back with you? And look at your hands!

Macbeth: There is blood on my hands. I am stunned by tonight's events and cannot seem to move properly.

Lady Macbeth: Do not be such a ridiculous fool!

Macbeth: Last night, I heard a voice cry out, "Sleep no more! Macbeth does murder sleep!" I will be haunted by last night's events forever. I will never again have a peaceful night's sleep.

Lady Macbeth: You must act in haste. Wash your bloodstained hands while I position the dagger near the guards. Hurry, I hear someone coming.

Macbeth: You are right, I must pull myself together. I will wash this blood from my hands and answer the door.

Macduff: Good morning, Macbeth.

Macbeth: Oh, good morning, Macduff. I did not hear you come in. What brings you to Inverness at such an early hour?

Macduff: Good morning, Lady Macbeth.

Lady Macbeth: Oh, good morning, Macduff. What a pleasant surprise. I did not know you were here.

Macduff: I am sorry to arrive here so early, but I am sick with worry. The very order of the world seems overthrown.

Lady Macbeth: What do you mean, Macduff?

Macduff:	Bizarre things are happening all over the kingdom. Birds and horses are dying for no reason. I fear for the life of our beloved King Duncan, for when nature revolts against itself, it means no good for us.
Macbeth:	There is no need to worry about the king's safety. But if it will make you feel better, let us wake him and you can see for yourself that he is fine.
Macduff:	Yes, I must see him to ease my worries.
Macbeth:	This way to his chamber, Macduff.
Macduff:	Oh no, what is this I see? The king has been murdered in cold blood!
Macbeth:	I cannot believe my eyes! This is an outrage, a travesty against the natural order of things. Our beloved king is dead! Every soul who breathes will be questioned. Sound the bell!
Lady Macbeth:	I cannot believe this has happened in our castle. Oh, everyone is coming in now to see King Duncan. Malcolm and Donalbain, I fear your father, our great king, has been murdered. Oh, I feel faint!

Macbeth: Lady Macbeth has fainted. Get the chambermaid to help her. I want to see every man in the great hall right now to discuss what is to be done!

Malcolm: My brother and I will stay here with our father.

Macbeth: All right, but the rest of you come with me now.

Malcolm: Something is not right. I will not meet with these men when I know one of them murdered our father. You can be certain that whoever murdered him will want our deaths, as well. I will go to England and build an army. Donalbain, go pursue our interests in Ireland. I will write soon.

Act II, Scene III

Later in the great hall at Macbeth's castle

Macbeth: Look out the window! See Malcolm and Donalbain fleeing. They must have murdered their father. They are his immediate heirs and stand to profit the most from his untimely death.

Banquo: I see your point Macbeth, but I am filled with worry.

Macbeth: Now that Malcolm and Donalbain have fled, the seat of the king is left vacant. We must choose a new king tonight before the country falls into chaos.

Banquo: You have fought most bravely, Macbeth. You should definitely be king.

Macduff: We should not act in such haste. The king does have his own heirs.

Banquo: Nonsense, Macduff. King Duncan's sons are his murderers. We cannot reward them after the dreadful deed they committed. Macbeth is a hero, and he must now be our king.

Macbeth: Thank you, Banquo. I accept the honor to be king, although my joy is tainted with the sadness of Duncan's untimely murder.

Act III, Scene I

A few days later at the Palace of Dunsinane

Macbeth: Banquo, I will be having a great feast here at Dunsinane tonight in honor of my rise to the throne. It seems that the witches' prophecies are coming true, after all.

Banquo: Macbeth, my good friend, the first two of the witches' prophecies have come to pass. But for the third, they said my heir would be king, and that is not possible now that you wear the crown.

Macbeth: Your son, Fleance, is a very fine young man, but I am afraid that what you say is true. Fleance cannot be king if I am king. Speaking of your son, are you going riding this afternoon with him?

Banquo: Yes, we will ride together to the river.

Macbeth: Good. Enjoy your ride, and be sure to bring your son to the royal feast here this evening. Goodbye, Banquo.

Banquo: I will. Goodbye.

Macbeth: Banquo is a threat to me. It is for this reason that he and Fleance must die today. I have hired their murderers and wait for the confirmation of their deaths. Lady Macbeth knows nothing of this plan, which is best. Ah, here she comes now.

Lady Macbeth: My good husband, you seem so downtrodden. We have a great feast tonight, and you must not appear so sad. Our guests depend on your joyous company, for you are now their king.

Macbeth: I have much on my mind right now. But do not worry, all will be well. I await some news. Let me take my leave.

Lady Macbeth: What news? We always share our thoughts be they for good or for bad, and I must know what is wrong.

Macbeth: It is nothing important. Do not worry needlessly, Lady Macbeth, it is of no concern to you. Now you must ready yourself for tonight's celebration.

Lady Macbeth: All right, my husband, but what you are saying does not sit well with me.

Poem: Sonnet 150

Act III, Scene II

Royal celebration at the Palace of Dunsinane

Lady Macbeth: My lord, all of the guests have arrived, so please be of good cheer.

Macbeth: All of the guests are not here. Where are Banquo and his son, Fleance?

Lady Macbeth: Were you sleeping? Have you not heard the news? Banquo was murdered on his way here.

Macbeth: What about Fleance?

Lady Macbeth: He escaped.

Macbeth: Escaped? Really? I, I, I…do not understand. I am not feeling well.

Lady Macbeth: Pull yourself together! You have guests to entertain.

Banquo: Yes, you understand. Look at these bloody hands, Macbeth. My blood is upon your soul.

Macbeth: No! It cannot be you. I cannot be talking to a ghost. Do not shake your bloody hands at me.

Lady Macbeth: What is happening? The guests are beginning to talk about your strange actions.

Macbeth: Do you not see him? There he stands, the ghost of Banquo. Get out! I took care of you today. Your blood is cold!

Lady Macbeth: Stop it!

Macduff: What is happening? I do not like hearing Macbeth rail like this. He seems almost insane.

Lady Macbeth: What are you saying, Macduff?

Macduff: I can no longer serve him. I shall go to England and find Malcolm.

Macbeth: You will *what*? Get out, you horrible shadow! Quit my sight!

Lady Macbeth: Honored and respected guests, do not mind what my husband is saying, it is nothing. Do not worry, for he is sometimes like this when he does not get enough sleep. (*whispering*) Husband, do sit and relax—you are scaring everyone.

Macbeth: It will have blood: blood will have blood. We will pay for what we have done!

Lady Macbeth: (*whispering*) Please calm down, my love, for people are starting to wonder whether you are fit to serve as king.

| Macbeth: | I must go now and visit with the witches to ask for their wisdom to comfort me. It was their prophecies that brought me to this place, and it will be their words that I will use to keep me here. |

Act IV, Scene 1

Later that night outside

| Witches: | By the pricking of my thumbs, something wicked this way comes. Ah, it is Macbeth. |

| Macbeth: | I come to you and command you to answer the questions that I have. |

| Witches: | We know why you are here, Macbeth, and will answer with our breath. Double, double toil and trouble, fire burn and cauldron bubble. Cool it with a baboon's blood, then the charm is firm and good. |

| Macbeth: | I just want to ask… |

| Witches: | Say no more is what you should do. The answer will come, but it will not be commanded by you. Beware Macduff! Beware Macduff! But that is not enough. |

Macbeth:	Why Macduff?
Witches:	Be bloody, bold, and resolute; laugh to scorn the power of man, for you will not be harmed by any man born of a woman.
Macbeth:	You speak in riddles. What do you mean? If no man can harm me, then why should I fear Macduff?
Witches:	Hush and be still, for more news comes to you. Macbeth shall never be vanquished until the Great Birnam Wood comes to Dunsinane Hill.
Macbeth:	What are you saying? Birnam Wood is next to my palace, and everyone knows that trees cannot move. Everyone also knows that all men are born of woman. Does that mean that Dunsinane is safe?
Witches:	Beware, Macbeth, beware! The new line of kings shall come from your friend Banquo's heirs.
Macbeth:	This is mockery and foolishness.
Witches:	That this great king may kindly say, our duties did his welcome pay.

Macbeth: Where have they gone? The witches have disappeared. I am confused by their warning, "Beware Macduff." Macduff has refused to serve me and is now traveling to England. I am so enraged that I will stop by his castle this very night and murder his family. That should get his attention!

Act IV, Scene II

Macduff's home in England

Malcolm: I am glad to see you here, Macduff. I am privileged that you join forces with me.

Macduff: Macbeth has become an evil man, Malcolm. The power of the throne has changed him. He once was honorable, courageous, and loyal. But now he is consumed by power and fear.

Malcolm: Power does corrupt men. I worry about it myself, as I am the true heir to the throne since my father's murder.

Macduff: We must fight Macbeth! If we do not, he will ruin the country.

Malcolm:	I fear you are right. But wait, what is that I hear? Someone is knocking at the door. Wait here, Macduff, for it will only take a minute. Macduff, it was a messenger with appalling news for you.
Macduff:	What is it? Tell me.
Malcolm:	Macbeth laid siege to your home and murdered everyone. He spared no one. Your wife, your children, and your servants are all dead.
Macduff:	My family murdered? My wife? My little children?
Malcolm:	Turn your anger into resolve to fight! I have gathered an army here in England. We must return to challenge Macbeth. I will send word to Donalbain to meet us there with his army. Together, we can kill Macbeth.

Act V, Scene 1

At the Palace of Dunsinane

Lady Macbeth:	Oh, I am plagued by such horrific nightmares and hallucinations. Out, damned spot! Out I say! Will these hands ever be clean? I wash them, I perfume them, and still they drip with blood. What's done cannot be undone.

Macbeth: Your sanity seems to be vanishing quickly, my wife. Take hold of yourself! I hear someone at the door. Go to bed and get some rest.

Lady Macbeth: Yes, sleep. That would be good.

Macbeth: Ah, messenger. What news do you have for me. What? Malcolm, Macduff, and their armies are coming from England? Ha! What have I to fear, for they can never win!

Act V, Scene II
England

Malcolm: I have a plan, Macduff. One that I am confident will work.

Macduff: What is it, Malcolm?

Malcolm: Macbeth will be watching for us, so we must disguise ourselves. We can cut the branches off of the trees in Birnam Wood and each man can carry a branch in front of him to hide his body. This way, we will be able to get close to the castle without detection.

| Macduff: | That is brilliant, Malcolm. I am ready. Let us return to Scotland. |

Act V, Scene III

The Palace of Dunsinane

| Macbeth: | Lady Macbeth, I need to speak to you. Why do you lie there so still and lifeless, like a frozen statue? Oh, no! She is dead! I knew you were fragile, my love, but I never expected suicide! Out, out, brief candle! Life is but a walking shadow, a poor player that struts and frets his hour upon the stage and then is heard no more. And now, what is this I see outside? How can this be? It seems as if the trees of Birnam Wood are marching toward Dunsinane. Oh, no! The witches' prophecies are coming true. |

| Malcolm: | We are near the castle now, Macduff. |

| Macduff: | Yes, we can storm the castle. There is that coward, Macbeth. I will fight him to his death! |

| Macbeth: | Your effort is wasted, Macduff, for I can only be harmed by a man who was not born of a woman. |

Macduff: Then you have met him this day Macbeth, for I was not born of woman; I was untimely ripped from my mother's womb. Surrender, Macbeth, your time as false king is up!

Macbeth: I will never yield my crown in this life. I have fought and taken this crown for my own, and I will not give it up, even on the brink of death.

Macduff: You had no right to the throne or to the lives of my family. You will now pay dearly for all your evil deeds. You have shown me no mercy, and thus, I will show you no mercy. Die, you dirty scoundrel! There, I have beheaded the false king. Malcolm, I give you Macbeth's head to do with as you wish.

Malcolm: Let us rejoice, for this time of violence and evil is over. We will begin to heal the wounds inflected by this butcher, Macbeth, and his evil wife. All who stood with me today shall be rewarded. I now invite everyone to see me crowned at Scone.

Song: Sonnet 33

Sonnet 150

William Shakespeare

O, from what power hast thou this powerful might

With insufficiency my heart to sway,

To make me give the lie to my true sight,

And swear that brightness doth not grace the day?

Whence hast thou this becoming of things ill,

That in the very refuse of thy deeds

There is such strength and warrantise of skill

That in my mind thy worst all best exceeds?

Who taught thee how to make me love thee more,

The more I hear and see just cause of hate?

O, though I love what others do abhor,

With others thou shouldst not abhor my state.

     If thy unworthiness raised love in me,

     More worthy I to be beloved of thee.

Sonnet 33

William Shakespeare

Full many a glorious morning have I seen

Flatter the mountain tops with sovereign eye,

Kissing with golden face the meadows green,

Gilding pale streams with heavenly alchemy;

Anon permit the basest clouds to ride

With ugly rack on his celestial face,

And from the forlorn world his visage hide,

Stealing unseen to west with this disgrace:

Even so my sun one early morn did shine

With all-triumphant splendour on my brow;

But, out, alack, he was but one hour mine,

The region cloud hath masked him from me now.

    Yet him for this my love no whit disdaineth:

    Suns of the world may stain when heaven's sun staineth.

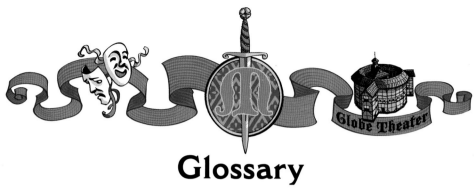

Glossary

abhor—to shrink from in disgust

alchemy—a medieval chemical science

ambition—an eager desire for power, fame, or to achieve a particular goal

decreed—decided by or ordered by an authority figure

entices—attracts by arousing hope or desire

forlorn—sad and lonely; feeling near hopelessness

hallucinations—to have the awareness of things that seems to be experienced through one of the senses but is not real

insufficiency—the lack of something

Middle Ages—the period of European history from about AD 500–1500

mockery—an insulting action or speech

prophecy—the foretelling of the future

remorse—a deep regret coming from having done something wrong

thane—a lord in Scotland during the Middle Ages

trepidation—a state of alarm or nervousness

utterances—manners or styles of speaking; or things spoken

visage—an expression of the face

whit—smallest part imaginable